SEVEN WONDERS JOURNALS

⨟ THE ⨟ KEY

SEVEN WONDERS JOURNALS

THE
KEY

BY PETER LERANGIS

HARPER
An Imprint of HarperCollinsPublishers

Seven Wonders Journals: The Key

Library of Congress catalog card number: 2014942409
ISBN 978-0-06-223892-4

Typography by Joseph Merkel
14 15 16 17 18 OPM 10 9 8 7 6 5 4 3 2 1
❖
First Edition

⚡THE⚡
KEY

PRIVATE JOURNAL

ALIYAH BARTEVYAN

(Osman, if you are even breathing within three feet of this, I will personally bash your head and rip up every Beatles poster you own!!!!!)

Tuesday, 11:00 P.M.

DIARY, I'M HAVING a bad night. My head is full of the Most-Girls thoughts. As in, Most Girls my age don't live in a dirt hole like mine. Most Girls don't live in shacks with stolen electricity via a rat-eaten wire from a neighbor. Most Girls go to school, buy nice clothes, read good books, help their mother with housework, take care of a pet.

I, Diary, as you know, am not Most Girls.

My school is the Khalid Bartevyan School of Crazy. I have no regular bedtime. My clothes and books come

1

from other people's trash. The clothes I hate, the books I like. Right now I am reading *American History from 1776 to Now*, but every page is missing after about 1910. With Mother gone, housework is optional, and the last pet I had was MoopaSoopa, that fat, snuggly rat who followed Father home from an exploration and met an untimely death by chewing through a live electrical wire.

Well, I have a pet now. Sort of. Her name is Safi, she's a ferret my father borrowed for his latest scheme, and she's about as snuggly as a drawer full of needles. But she has . . . Magical Properties! She will sniff out Treasures Untold from Hidden Places! She is a Millionaire Maker!

Do you believe that, Diary? I don't. But Father does, of course. Safi is the latest scheme that is going to make us Rich, Rich, Rich!

Ughhh . . .

Do you know how Father described himself today? As a "Chief Officer of Bartevyan Antiquities Incorporated, Salvage Specialists." Can you believe that? Bartevyan Antiquities? Some officer—he's more of a Chief Babysitter to those four or five slovenly, useless men he works with. They come to our house, and when they leave, Father's bottles are mostly empty.

Ah well, I don't suppose he can say "Chief Tomb Robber of a Group of Jobless Drunks." It doesn't have the same ring.

But back to Safi. I do not like her. Or her owner, a wealthy one-eyed man named Feyyaz the Cyclops—who, by the way, is not snuggly either. They say his missing eye was taken in a rare playful moment by Safi. What Feyyaz lacks in looks, he makes up for in money—and nastiness. No one ever calls him Cyclops to his face, of course. It is said he once chopped off a man's fingers for shaking his hand without bowing first.

Father will not tell us how Feyyaz got his wealth. Or how he got his charming personality or unique odor. Or why on earth he lent Safi to us.

Does Feyyaz really believe we will find a hidden ancient treasure? I worry he expects us to fail—and then he'll blackmail us with something or other. Given Father's track record, what else could he be thinking????

I know, Diary, if you were not a book, you would slap me—for being so disrespectful. And I would deserve it. But I can't help but think there is something foul afoot.

I can't really complain to Osman. Whenever I try, he looks at me as if I've grown donkey ears. He thinks our life is perfect. Sometimes I can't believe he and I are twins. He seems so much younger than me. In fact, he believes in this Safi nonsense! Argghhh! (Well, he also believes that the TV sitcom *I Dream of Jeannie* is a documentary and that Father is a serious archaeologist.)

Both of the men in my life confuse reality and fantasy.

I'm Mother's daughter, Diary—strong, practical, loyal, smart, modest, AND IF ANYONE EVER STEALS THIS DIARY AND REPEATS THAT CONCEITED-SOUNDING STATEMENT, I WILL PERSONALLY VANQUISH YOU, AND THAT ESPECIALLY INCLUDES MY SNEAK OF A BROTHER KNOWN AS OSMAN!

Sorry, had to include that disclaimer.

Mother always said Father's stories would get us in trouble. "Just find a job, Khalid," she would tell him. "Ordinary people don't chase after treasure. Ordinary people have jobs."

"Who wants to be ordinary?" was his response.

He had a point. But so did she. I miss Mother sooooo much, Diary.

Last night I dreamed about her. Again. Which is what I wanted to write about. Because I am still shaking and I do not think I shall ever sleep again.

Wednesday, 12:09 A.M.

SORRY. HAD TO put you away. Father fell off the bed and I had to wake him up, which took a while.

Where was I?

Oh, yes, the dream.

Okay, all I saw was Mother's back. She was walking

4

along the shore, wearing a long, brocaded gown. I shouted to her but she didn't turn around. No! Her pace picked up . . . and she was headed directly into the sea. Of course I followed, screaming at the top of my lungs, trying to pull her away, but she wouldn't even turn to face me. Next thing I knew, we were both underwater.

Diary, I was breathing—and nothing scared me! Not even the eels and jellyfish (who you know I hate with a passion)! They were tickling me like the softest feathers as I walked along the ocean bottom. I could hear a voice, coming from Mother, saying over and over . . .

"You have such a strong soul, my dear . . ."

"You have such a strong soul, my dear . . ."

Strong soul? Really? I giggled. It sounded like one of the scary voices Mother used when telling us ghost stories. When I finally caught up to her, I tugged on her hand. "Where are we going?" I asked.

My fingers slid away. The skin had just . . . slipped off like dried masking tape. I sprang back, holding it in my fingertips. I wanted to scream, but no sound came out.

Then she turned. It wasn't Mother at all, but a haggard old witch with a mummy's face and a smile like a stab wound. "Let me see the back of your head, my dearie," she said, as if that made perfect sense.

I couldn't answer. My mouth just flapped open and shut like a fish.

"Do you have it?" Her voice was growing less patient, sharper.

"Have . . . what?" I asked.

I backed away, shaking my head. I didn't know what she meant. Before I could run, she grabbed my arm, turned me around, and let out a shriek . . .

The next thing I knew, Father was shaking me awake. His eyes were bloodshot and desperate. Osman, of course, was fast asleep. But there was someone else in the room—Father's ugly friend, Gencer. I could recognize him even in the dark. His back is curved like an S, and one tuft of hair juts from his head like a sprig of scorched grass.

I caught my breath. That thing was not Mother . . . that thing was not Mother . . . that thing was not Mother . . . I repeated to myself over and over.

I thought about Mother's smile. I thought about the way she could make Father—all of us—happy.

Then I thought about how much she disliked Gencer. How she'd banned him from our house. "What are you doing here?" I asked, gathering up my courage.

Old Gencer leaned forward, into the light that reflected off the wall from Father's flashlight. As always, his face was twisted in agony, as if he'd bitten down on a razor blade. "Either the girl is possessed," he said, "or she ate your cooking last night, Khalid. Heh! Now be silent, girl. How can you expect a man to think in peace . . ."

He turned to leave, waving a half-empty bottle, before falling down and passing out at the doorstep. And I realized he hadn't said the word *think* after all, but a much uglier word that rhymes with it. And begins with *dr*.

Wednesday, 1:00 A.M.

RAKI.

No, whiskey.

No, raki.

Father is curled up on the floor, snoring. Each of his breaths wafts over me like a gust from a drainage pipe. I'm pretty sure it's raki, because of the faint licorice smell.

I used to like licorice. But not anymore. I have smelled it one too many times in our shack, in the form of a foul alcoholic drink that changes Father's personality.

Yup, still awake, Diary. Will this night ever end??? In a few hours, just after sunrise, we go to the beautiful city of Fethiye on another Great Adventure—a search for the Missing Ring of the Great King Harpagus of Lycia. Apparently it is worth gazillions.

Wait, you say, there are holes in this logic! Well, yes. First of all Harpagus was not a king, because Lycia was not its own country—part of the Persian Empire, technically. So he was technically a satrap. A lesser ruler. Second, no one knows where this ring is, or if it ever existed at all.

And that is where Safi the Magical Ferret comes in. She will find the Ring That May Not Ever Have Been, which belonged to the Guy Who Was Not a King. And we will live happily ever after.

Is this just insane? Have we heard this kind of story before?

Yes. Last month it was missing pinkie of the Statue of Zeus from Olympia. Six weeks ago it was King Tut's mustache. Three months ago, Cleopatra's golden toenail clippers.

All wild-goose chases.

Okay, I admit, I'm a little excited. I have never been to Fethiye but it sounds wonderful, all beaches and seaside cafés. Whoa, here come the Most-Girl thoughts, as in when Most Girls go to the beach with their fathers, they're not robbing tombs with a smelly ferret. Of course, Osman says

Sorry, Diary, had to put you away for a few minutes. Father woke up. I think he saw you. You know what he said to me? "Aliyah, promise me you will keep your brother safe."

I didn't know what to say. "Of course I will," I stammered. "Why do you—?"

"He will be a great man," he said. "But his soul is wild, untamed, and incautious. And you will need him someday . . ."

I was on the verge of saying *So what am I, chopped liver?* when he smiled, and his eyes seemed to gain a sharp focus I hadn't seen since Mother died.

". . . Because you, my daughter," he said, "you will save the world . . ."

At that last word, his eyes closed and he drifted to sleep.

I am smiling now. Sometimes Father's dreams reveal the foolishness in his head but also the love in his heart.

I think I will sleep now, Diary.

Wednesday, 10:32 P.M.

UCCCH. SORRY, DIARY, for the coffee stain.

Yes, yes, I know, I hate coffee. But as the others yammer and argue around the fire, I need to stay awake and write down what happened today. Because I am worried about all of us.

We set off shortly after dawn. Osman was the only one wide awake. He sang a horrible little song called the "Hunt for the Ring of Asparagus" to the tune of "Davy Crockett, King of the Wild Frontier." I thought Gencer would clock him over the head. I (almost) wouldn't have minded.

We were trudging up a hill to find the ruined tomb where the ring was supposed to be hidden. Gencer was huffing and puffing, a cigar dangling from his lip. (Father buys the cigars, of course, even though Gencer is the only one who smokes them.) "So when that wretched animal finds the ring," Gencer grumbled, watching Safi relieve herself in the middle of the trail, "then what? Maybe we can use our profits to invest in an oracular animal of our very own! Maybe, say, a three-legged goat who will eat its way to the Holy Grail?" He blew our way a puff of cigar smoke that smelled like someone had replaced the tobacco with manure.

"Have a little faith, my wise and wizened incompetent," Father said.

Gencer looked momentarily confused (as he usually does when Father uses words of two syllables or more), then quickly regained his sarcasm. "You know, Khalid," he finally said, "there was a time when you had a knack for finding a little something here and there, but this ferret business makes me think you're just grasping at straws."

"Ah," Father replied. "And you, of course, have a better idea. Like your splendid scheme to pose as a statue by painting yourself silver, thereby suffocating yourself in public—"

"I was younger then!" Gencer snapped, wincing at the memory. "I do have an idea, you know. And it's far better than this elongated rat—"

Safi let out an angry-sounding chitter, as if she'd understood. Father cut Gencer off with a wave of his hand. We watched as Safi sniffed the air. Tail twitching, she disappeared into the side of the mountain.

"You see, my disgruntled simian friend, she's caught the scent!" Father looked triumphantly at Gencer.

"Looks to me like she's running away," he grunted. Then quietly he turned toward Osman and me. "What does *simian* mean?"

"Apelike," I said.

"It's a compliment," Osman lied.

Before Gencer could formulate a reply, Safi emerged from a dark, narrow gap in the rocks—with a little brown vole twitching between her teeth. I winced and turned away.

Gencer let out a bellowing laugh. "Well, look at that! She found a ferret restaurant! Ha! Some treasure hunter!"

Safi turned and dropped the vole at Gencer's feet. The old slob screamed like a baby, dropping the half-smoked, saliva-soaked cigar to the ground. "Khalid, you owe me a fresh cigar!"

But Osman and I were eyeing the gap Safi had found. It was just about as wide as Osman was, and maybe a foot high.

"Wow," Osman said—and just like that, he slipped inside, vanishing into the blackness.

"Osman!" Father shouted. "Get back here at once!"

"What do you think you're doing?" I added, grabbing Father's flashlight. I peered into the opening, gauging whether I could fit in myself. I could make out a wide, low cave, cool as death.

But no Osman.

"Like father, like son," Gencer muttered, with a superior little chortle. "No common sense."

Father wheeled on his friend, grabbing him by the collar. But as he pulled Gencer toward him, a muffled scream came up from the opening.

Osman.

My heart jumped into my mouth. We all screamed his name now, even Gencer. "I'm going in," I said.

"No," Father replied, grabbing my arm.

I knew he wanted to go in himself, but there was no way he'd fit. I squeezed my head into the gap . . . then my shoulders . . .

Fingers closed around my upper arm. I lurched back, squashing my head into the top of the gap. "Father!"

"BWAH-HA-HA-HA!" cackled a voice.

A shrill, little-boy voice.

I blinked my eyes, fighting back pain. And anger. "Osman, you little creep, that wasn't funny!"

Luckily I had enough presence of mind to yank him out of the opening. He tumbled to the ground, giggling hysterically.

That was when I saw Gencer, flat on his back. He had fainted at the sound of the scream. Judging from Safi's angry scolding noises, he had also landed directly on top of the now-dead vole.

I wanted to strangle Osman for scaring me. Father's eyes were bulging in anger. But I knew both of us felt too much relief, too much joy at the fact that Osman was alive.

Diary, he gets away with murder. Really.

Of course Osman ignored our scolding. His eyes dancing, he grabbed the flashlight and swung the beam inside, illuminating the small cave. "Look at this, *Baba*!" he said. "Don't be mad—just look! Some ferret restaurant!"

At that, Gencer stirred. When he saw Safi perched angrily on his chest, he jumped to his feet. None of us paid much attention to his bloodcurdling scream when he realized he'd passed out on a dead vole.

Father, Osman, and I were busy peering inside the gap. It led to a cavernous room, the walls smooth and dry, the floor only a short drop from the opening.

For once, I thought, we might be on to something.

Osman and I looked at Father. He thought a moment, then nodded tentatively. I gave him my most confident look. "You always told us, *Baba*, the biggest part of Bartevyan is Brave . . ."

"And the biggest part of Gencer," Osman added, glancing toward Father's sidekick, who now looked sick to his stomach, "is Green."

Father smiled for the first time all morning. Quickly Osman and I slipped through the opening and dropped to the floor. The air inside was cool and delicious after the long hike. Thousands of tiny glints in the walls shone in Osman's flashlight beam. He pointed the light toward the back of the room, toward a passage that led deeper into the mountain.

As we walked, a thick silence fell over us like a fog. As smooth as the walls of the cave were, the rock along the passageway was rough, covered with herky-jerky gashes and cracks. At the far end, Osman and I reached another opening, this one as small as the gap we'd slipped through. It led into solid blackness.

"Father! There's a hidden tunnel down here!" Osman crowed, his voice echoing along the walls.

From high above, Father whooped loud enough for us to hear. "God lord, Safi did it! She led us to our starting point. You'll be safe down there?"

I saw Father shudder as a rope-like shape leaped onto the floor.

Safi.

"Our fearless leader is here," I said. "We're in good paws."

Father tossed down another flashlight, which I caught. "We'll be waiting on the other side," he said. "We'll see you when you come out with the treasure!"

He was trying to sound trusting and confident. But he didn't fool me.

SORRY, HAD TO settle an argument over who drank Gencer's raki. The answer was Safi. She is, as you can imagine, fast asleep. Okay, where was I?

Right. This morning in the tunnel.

So I scampered ahead of Osman, swinging my flashlight from side to side. I ducked my head to avoid stalactites; the uneven walls scraped my elbows.

Being shorter, Osman should have had an easier time, but he fell behind, screaming in his bravest Bartevyan voice, "Hey, wait up!"

Safi peeked her head out of my jacket. "It's okay, Safi," I said. "We'll slow down. My little brother is investigating secret codes in the walls. Or maybe he's just afraid."

"Little brother?" echoed Osman's voice. "In case you missed that day in biology, twins means born at the same time."

"In case you missed that day in common sense, that is physically impossible," I replied. "I was born ten minutes earlier."

"Wow," Osman said. "I wonder what it'll feel like when I'm that old, Safi."

Osman pushed past and stomped ahead of me in the dark. His flashlight beam flitted across the walls, then disappeared. I rounded a corner and saw him, standing still in

15

the center of a large cavern.

"Unbelievable . . . ," he said in a hushed voice.

"What?" I asked.

He turned to me, his eyes wide. "It's ten minutes later and it feels exactly the same."

Diary, would it be wrong for a girl to wring her brother's neck?

I arced my flashlight around the massive chamber. Scenes from old battles played themselves out on the walls in faded blacks, yellows, blues, reds—bearded soldiers brandishing spears, a winged woman holding a yellow ball of fire, and a square-jawed king wearing a glorious robe and holding an ornate staff topped by an inverted triangle.

I let out a gasp. Osman was slack-jawed. "Father was right," he said. "This is the Big One! This is it!"

His flashlight played along one of the walls. At the base of a flaking image were dark, charcoal lines. Some kind of writing. "I think I can read this . . . ," Osman said in a hushed voice. "Those books we picked up from the library trash . . . one of them was about hieroglyphics and runes . . ."

Osman leaned closer, moving his lips silently. "What does it say?" I asked.

"'The Ring of . . . Har . . . pay . . . Harpagus,'" he exclaimed with glee, ". . . shall be revealed to the firstborn son of the Lord of Antiquities, known to all as Osman the Wise, ruler of his sister, Aliyah the Lame and Half-Witted . . ."

I would have bopped his head with the flashlight if it weren't trained on something against the opposite wall—three large wooden rectangular containers, leaning up against the rock. I moved closer, running the light up and down rotting, ancient planks with faded traces of rich decoration. "Coffins . . . ," I murmured.

"Smells more like tea," Osman said.

"Not coffee, coffins—look!" I said.

Osman's face fell. "Okay, this isn't a treasure room, it's a grave. And we're after money, not mummies."

"Where do you think treasures were buried?" I said. "With the dead! Maybe King Harpagus was buried here!"

"He wasn't a king, he was a rattrap," Osman said meekly. "You said so."

"Satrap," I corrected him. "Maybe Safi sniffed out Harpagus, lying in there with his ring still on his finger."

"Finger bone . . . ," Osman said.

"Are you afraid?" I asked, stepping into the room.

"Not if you go first." Osman's face had lost its color, but his curiosity was getting the better of him. He followed me into a dank, musty room, its air acrid and freezing cold. "What's that smell?"

"Vole poop," I said with a shrug. "Or maybe bat."

"Stop it!" Osman said, still staring at the coffins. "You're forcing out the *Brave* from Bartevyan! You're leaving just the . . ." He thought a moment. "*Tyan!*"

But I was training my flashlight at the ceiling, to a small recess, partway up the wall—a squarish natural shelf formed by the rock. In it, I could make out a dark, rectangular shape about a foot long. "What's that?" I asked.

Osman gulped. "Doesn't exactly scream 'This is a ring box!' to me," he said.

"But if it is," I said, "we wouldn't have to disturb the Addams Family over there, against the wall."

"Good point!" Osman stood under the recess, knelt, and braced his hands against the wall. "You go first. On my shoulders. Don't say I never helped you out."

"Can you hold my weight?" I asked.

"Depends on how much filet mignon you ate last night," he said as I cautiously stepped onto his shoulder.

The walls were freezing cold, and sparkles of frost danced on the stone in front of me. My eyes barely reached the opening.

I fished out my flashlight and thrust it forward. The beam lit up a small carved stone box, covered in symbols that resembled the ones on the walls. I reached forward to take it, my head echoing with Father's favorite words, "Trust me, Aliyah . . ."

Something was scrabbling against my stomach. I nearly fell.

Safi.

Her pinprick claws danced up my sleeve, and in an instant she was climbing onto the ledge. Pain shot up my arm, and I let out an involuntary yelp. Safi squeaked and threw herself backward over my face, her claws buried in my scalp. My arms windmilled as I tried to get my balance back. I reached upward. Clasping the box, I toppled off Osman's shoulders.

I hit the ground with a thump. I blinked my eyes to see Osman standing over me, his flashlight trained on the box, which lay on my chest.

"What's inside it?" he asked.

"I'm fine, thank you very much!" I snapped.

He was already on his knees, reaching for the box. "Ali, you're a genius. We're rich. We'll split this fifty-fif—"

As he flung open the lid of the box, a musty smell wafted out. Osman's face went slack.

Inside the chest was a skeletal hand with nothing but wisps of leathery skin hanging off its bony fingers. No ring in sight.

I didn't feel disgust, Diary. I'd been here too many times before. Looking for treasure only to find junk. Father and his stupid schemes!

"I guess someone took the ring but left the hand!" I started to slam the chest shut.

"Yeeeow!" Osman cried out, jerking his hand away. "Are

you trying to leave my hand in there, too?"

"Sorry!" I felt awful. I should never let my anger get the better of me.

Grimacing, Osman staggered backward, toward the opposite wall. Toward the coffins. "Osman, careful—"

Too late. His back connected with the tallest box. The fragile, rotted wood splintered with a dry *crrraaack*.

I watch in horror as Osman and the coffin toppled together to the floor in a cloud of splintering wood and bone. I felt light-headed. My little brother was screaming, rigid, lying in the embrace of a grinning skeleton. As Osman flailed, his feet twisted in the splintered wood, the skeleton moved with him as if it were alive.

"Aliyah, help me!" he cried.

So what did I do, dear Diary? What heroic act? I stood there like a mannequin, frozen, doing nothing—until I noticed a set of furry, jointed black legs crawling up my brother's calves.

Finally I leaped forward and kicked at them, sending a black shape flying into the darkness. Osman jumped, disentangling himself, staggering, doubled over with nausea.

Now I could see a huge black spider—easily the size of my hand—scurrying out from beneath the skeleton. It was followed by another . . . and another . . .

"Look out!" I shouted, yanking my brother away by the arm. The spiders scurried away on all eights. I heard a hissing noise and turned to see Safi scrabbling with another of the little beasts. I wasn't sure if she wanted to bat it away or eat it. I stomped on one spider and flicked another off Osman's knee. We both began dancing frantically through the chamber, squashing spiders the size of rodents. I felt each one pulsing beneath the soles of my shoes.

As the last of the living spiders skittered away into the shadows I fought back the desire to puke. When I looked down I saw Osman had given in to his desire. We each swung our flashlights around the chamber. "Are you okay?" I asked.

Osman nodded. "Safi . . . ," he said, catching his breath. "What happened to the ferret?"

My flashlight beam caught a flash of white in the far corner of the chamber, by the floor. Safi's white, fluffy tail. It was just disappearing into a crack in the wall.

"No!" I groaned.

"W-we can't lose her," Osman said. "Feyyaz will be furious!"

I thought about Feyyaz chopping off the fingers of the man who hadn't sufficiently bowed to him. What would he do to someone who lost his ferret? I ran to the wall, lay flat on my belly, and thrust my hand into the small hole Safi had found. I felt it give a little and a few inches crumbled away. My fingers brushed Safi's fur, and I felt her leap backward. How much room did she have in there? I scraped at the edges of the hole I'd made, and more of the wall crumbled into my hand. Osman crouched next to me. "Safi! Come out!" he cooed. He knocked his fist against the wall.

A hollow thud echoed through the treasure chamber. Osman looked at me. "It's . . . plaster?" he said.

Without a word, we began pulling at it with our fingers. Plaster flaked off in great piles until we'd opened a space the size of our heads about an inch off the floor. Safi was on the other side, and she froze in the beams of our flashlights, looking relieved (as much as a ferret can, I guess).

Osman put his hand through the opening and pulled off one more great hunk of plaster. Our eyes met and we each grabbed the lip of the hole. I counted, "One, two, three!" We pulled together, and a square meter of the bottom of the wall came loose in a shower of dirt. There was an opening just high enough for us to crawl through—and a large, dark tunnel beyond.

Osman got on hands and knees, gathered Safi up into his jacket, and crawled through the tunnel opening. A blast of cold air hit me as I stood, shining my flashlight around. We followed this tunnel in a curved path until we reached a grand, ornate chamber, much bigger than the one we'd just left. The walls were adorned with statues of warriors on horseback, Greek gods with spears flying from their hands, and fantastic monsters. "How many rooms are there?" I asked.

"This one seems familiar," Osman said.

That was when I smelled coffee.

I switched off my flashlight. A line of bright light, like a yellow gash, shone into the room from our left. "Is that moonlight?" I asked.

"Is that coffee?" Osman said.

We ran across the chamber toward the sliver of light. It was coming through the crack of a doorway. Osman pushed it open, and the first thing I could see was a breathtaking view of Fethiye harbor. And not twenty meters away sat our father with Gencer. My heart nearly stopped when I saw who was with them—Feyyaz the Cyclops.

The men were warming their hands over a small fire, brewing coffee in an old tin pot. Father saw me first. "My chilrrren!" he said, staggering to his feet, smiling too broadly, walking too unsteadily.

I gave Osman a look. Drunk, I realized. They all were. Feyyaz must have brought a bottle. "You've found a way through!" Father continued, his eyes darting back toward the other men with fear and anticipation. "And of course you've brought me . . ."

His voice trailed off as Feyyaz approached. The man was easily twice my father's size. He was dressed in a cream-colored silk shirt and had several rings on his fat fingers. He wore no patch over his missing eye, which was permanently closed by an angry white scar.

23

"The jewel?" Feyyaz's voice was surprisingly high-pitched and hollow for a man his size, but his one good eye was trained on me like a gun. "The ring?"

"My children were guided by Safi!" Father blurted. "Whatever they accomplished or didn't was determined by the limits of Safi—"

"Dear Safi has no limits, isn't that right, my beautiful *kouklaki*?" Feyyaz's face suddenly twisted into a frightening, sour expression that may have been his version of fondness. He held out his arms toward the ferret.

Safi poked her head out of Osman's jacket and leaped to the floor. She began twitching and made a horrid hacking noise.

Feyyaz's eyes widened. He grabbed Father by his shirt front. "If those brats of yours have harmed my Safi, Khalid, you're a dead man!"

Safi gave an especially violent heave. Then she puked up the body of a mangled spider onto the floor of the tomb.

I picked up the spider, shaking with anger. I don't know what possessed me to do this, and looking back on it, it could have been suicide, but Most Girls don't usually witness their father being bullied and threatened by dangerous gangsters. Without a second thought I placed the spider in Feyyaz's outstretched hand. My voice was calm. "This is all we found, sir."

He squealed like one of my schoolmates and dropped it.

I grabbed Osman's hand and walked off, leaving my father and Feyyaz gawking.

Thursday, 8:03 A.M., in a Jeep (forgive the shaky handwriting, Diary)

"GET UP, ALIYAH."

Father.

"Osman! Up, up, up!"

Why was he whispering? I blinked my eyes open. It was still dark, my nose was cold. But at least I was alive. So was everyone. I guess Feyyaz wasn't in a murderous mood last night. He was preoccupied with Safi's health, nursing the little critter with mysterious, foul-smelling medicines that only seemed to make her worse. He fell asleep in the tent I'd pitched before the rest of us were even done setting up camp. He slept, snoring, with Safi in his beefy arms.

As Father shook us awake, I knew that was what he was thinking, too.

I could see Father's breath as well as smell it. He'd obviously stayed up most (or all) of the night, drinking with Gencer. I opened my mouth to speak, but Father put a finger to his lips. His eyes were red and watery, and kept flitting to the opening of our raggedy tent. "Let's go, children. Lots to do today," he said, trying to sound cheery.

Osman groaned. "What time is it?"

"Shhh!" Father said. "Uncle Feyyaz is still sleeping. He's had a rough night. Let's leave him in peace."

Uncle Feyyaz? Yes, Diary, that is what he said. Does Father think I don't know who Feyyaz is? Honestly, I've learned to let Father think he's fooling me. Sometimes it makes it easier to get what I want. But it was time for him to stop treating us like babies. "*Baba*, come on, you don't really think—" I began.

Osman slid out of his sleeping bag, yawning.

"Enough. Follow me now, before the Cyclops wakes." Father scooped up my sleeping bag with a shushing noise and hurried out to his old Jeep, leaving me sitting alone, on the ground, my mouth hanging open. It was the first time I'd ever heard him use that nickname.

And that is how I ended up here.

And why my handwriting is so shaky.

I must stop now. I shouldn't have written so much. More tomorrow. I am getting Jeepsick . . .

Thursday, 11:41 P.M.

CAN'T SLEEP AGAIN, Diary. Maybe it was the lingering effects of that horrible Jeep trip. I never want to ride in that godforsaken vehicle again. Gencer and Father sat in front, in the only seats, while Osman and I bundled with the bedrolls and equipment in the back. The roads seemed like they hadn't been paved since Harpagus's empire. When we got out, Osman rubbed his back and groaned like an old man. "That really is a rattrap," he grumbled.

Father still looked pale, glancing backward as if Feyyaz might mysteriously fly toward us.

"Don't worry, Khalid, that one-eyed fool will forget the whole thing the moment he wakes up," Gencer said, flicking another cigar impatiently to the ground. "Now, let me borrow this rust bucket for a few hours. I've got something I have to do."

"Borrow the Jeep?" Father said wearily. "Why?"

"It's called sharing—or am I supposed to buy a Cadillac from what we made yesterday?" Gencer replied, holding out his hand. "And, oh yes, I will need to buy gas, Khalid, unless you plan to push."

I glared at the old moocher, but Father just nodded, digging into his pocket.

As Gencer drove off, he grinned and stuck his tongue out at me, the creep. "Why do you let him boss you around like that?" I said. "Some bravery."

Osman glared at me, then put his arm around Father's shoulder and walked with him into our shack.

Diary, I felt terrible. *What are you doing, Aliyah?* I scolded myself. Father was tired. Defeated. I was not helping him by asking embarrassing questions! Feeling guilty, I went inside and fixed some lentil soup and bread. I served them

27

to Father, but he merely nibbled on the bread quietly and left his soup untouched. Finally he stood up and headed for the door, wiping his mouth. "Thank you, but I must go out. For . . . a meeting."

"You'll be back soon, right, *Baba*?" Osman asked, eyeing him warily.

"Of course. Take care of your sister," Father said as he pulled on his coat. Then his eyes briefly met mine. "You take care of your brother, too."

We watched him go. Again. To yet another mysterious "meeting." We were so used to this that it didn't seem strange at all. But I felt angry and confused. What kind of meeting does a tomb robber go to? Or was he just meeting up with Gencer and his friends at the tavern? Osman and I exchanged a glance without words. I don't know about other twins, but we can communicate with our eyes.

Once again, we had been the ones who had done the work. We had been in harm's way.

I sighed, turning back to do the dishes. For a change, Osman pitched in to help. "Do you think our luck will change?" I asked. "We haven't found much of anything in almost a month."

Osman shrugged. "It could be worse. We could have to go to school."

He had a point. In some ways I don't mind the life we lead. It's been ten months since I last went to school, but all I did there was argue with my teachers. They called me insubordinate, which means disobedient, but that is just not true. I am very respectful. I just speak up when people are wrong. I call that strong. And I can't help being that.

Anyway, now I like being able to explore the city, finding odd books to read, dodging truant officers. My life must seem pretty special to a normal schoolkid. But truly, Diary, if it meant I could have Mother back, I'd gladly go to school seven days a week and never talk back to a teacher ever again.

Friday, 12:26 A.M.

I CAN'T BELIEVE what just happened. My brain is racing. Father is back and he's fallen asleep for now, but I am worried for his life and I don't know what happened to Gencer or that horrible Greek man who—

Calm down, Aliyah.

One. Two. Three.

Okay.

Not long after my last entry, Diary, Father fell against the door and stumbled inside—right into the main room where my brother and I were sleeping. (Well, he was sleeping. I only pretended.)

I kept my eyes closed. I heard Father moving toward Osman and me. Behind my lids I could sense when he bent over me by the way the darkness got darker, if you know what I mean. A faint whiff of wine made me want to sneeze, but somehow I held still until he turned away.

He sat down at the table with a deep sigh, and I opened my eyes a crack. He looked very tired and old, sitting there.

But he nearly leaped off the bed at the sound of a sudden pounding at the door. So did I.

"Khalid!" a deep voice shouted from outside.

Father sprang up and hurried to the door. "Who's there?"

There was another thunderous blow on the door. The cheap lock tore out of the wood and the door swung inward.

I slitted my eyes wide enough to see what was happening. A man pushed into the room, shoving Father aside with one hand. The intruder was short and thickly built, with a mustache so big it covered his mouth. There was a knife in his belt, but I got the feeling he could do plenty of damage with his huge fists alone.

A second figure followed him—a skinny, cringing, weaselly man who could only be Gencer. As I lay there my hands curled into fists. Whatever was going on, Gencer was at the bottom of it.

"Feyyaz is not happy with you, Khalid," the man rumbled. "He knows what you did."

"What are you talking about?" Father said. "Knows what? Who are you?"

In a flash, the knife was in the man's hand. My breath caught.

"Call me Vasily the Greek," the man said. "Feyyaz believes you cheated him. Why else would you leave so suddenly? Your children found something in that tomb, didn't they? Feyyaz isn't so easily fooled."

As Vasily stepped closer, Father backpedaled, his hands in the air. "There wasn't anything in that tomb!" he pleaded. "I swear!"

Vasily went on as if Father hadn't even spoken, backing him up to the wall. "That stunt the girl pulled with the spider? That almost got you all killed right there, you know. You should be on your knees, grateful that Feyyaz is a man of mercy!" In a blindingly swift movement, he grabbed Father by the collar and pulled his face close. "And you know what's even worse? Feyyaz's beloved Safi is ruined."

"But—nothing happened to Safi!" Father said.

"She had the finest nose for precious metals of any ferret ever," Vasily went on. "But now she's depressed. She's not eating. She won't even look at a mousehole. Feyyaz says she is traumatized."

"A ferret—traumatized?" Father said.

Vasily nicked Father's cheek with the blade. I couldn't contain a gasp, but the man didn't care if I was asleep or awake. Father sank to the floor, his hand covering his face. "I—I will make amends!" he cried, as a tiny drop of blood ran down his chin. "I swear!"

"Yes, you will," Vasily hissed. "In fact, Feyyaz is thinking

31

twenty thousand will cover it. Barely."

"What?" Father blanched. "Twenty thousand lira is a lot of money!"

The man glared at Father. "Not lira. American dollars, you lowlife thief."

Twenty thousand dollars was a sum I couldn't even imagine! I thought Father was going to have a heart attack. "Gencer . . . ?" he said.

Gencer, hiding in the shadows, began backing toward the door. "I'll, um, just be going, then . . ."

Vasily whirled and pointed the knife at him. "Oh, don't think you're off the hook just because you showed me where Khalid lives. You're the one who got Feyyaz mixed up with this fool in the first place."

"Khalid begged me!" Gencer protested. "I tried to tell him Feyyaz was a busy man, but he wouldn't take no for an answer!"

"That's not true!" Father shot back.

As I lay there, watching, I felt my cheeks become hot. It was all I could do not to leap out of bed and start hitting Gencer with the broom. The spineless worm! The maggot! But to get to Gencer I'd have to deal with Feyyaz's hit man, and I'm not stupid. All I could do was lie still and try not to shake with rage. All I could think about was how Mother could make Gencer scuttle away like a frightened crab. I just know she would have handled

Vasily the Greek, that fat little gangster. But I am not Mother.

Vasily sighed and slung an arm around Father's shoulders. "Look. Between you and me, I really don't want to have to kill you and take your children to work for Feyyaz. It'll be so much easier if you just get the money."

Father nodded. "Yes. Yes, of course," he said. "I'll find it somehow. Tell Feyyaz not to worry."

The man let him go.

"You have one week," he said, and he and Gencer were gone.

Friday, 2:37 A.M.

I AM SO worried, Diary.

Gencer returned and woke up Father. They argued a bit, but after a few moments went out together. I called after him. I ran to the door. But he disappeared into the night, assuring me he would be safe.

Are any of us safe? Will we ever be again?

Friday, 1:09 P.M.

HE'S HOME.

He went right to bed.

I still smell licorice. I am sick to my stomach.

Saturday night

FINALLY A MOMENT of calm, without the earth shaking. Oh, right, I'll explain.

Osman and I spent the day yesterday cleaning up. We were too frightened to talk about what had happened. So we tried to joke. And reminisced about our old home, back when Mother was alive. Remember that little apartment with two bedrooms? It was THREE TIMES the size of our hovel now, and also three times as tidy. Oh, Diary, imagine what it would be like if we were still there. Osman and I would share a room, maybe even have bunking beds! We would keep it neat and cozy. We would have a pet dog.

We were arguing over a name for the dog—I wanted "King," but Osman insisted on "F'artagnan" (!!!!)—when Father pushed open the door. As it smacked against the wall, the ground shook. Hard.

Osman and I jumped back.

"Guess I don' know my own strength . . . ," Father grumbled. As he shuffled to the table, a cup began sliding toward him.

"*B-baba?*" Osman said.

Father stared at the cup, afraid to catch it. "Now?" he whispered as the cup slipped off the edge of the table. "Now that stinking ferret decides to perform magic?"

34

"It's not the ferret," I said. "Safi is not here, *Baba*. This is something else. This is . . ."

I didn't want to say. I wasn't sure, but I had an idea.

"Is what?" Osman demanded.

Cups and plates moving across surfaces, almost as if possessed. The earth, trembling!

"A foreshock," I said, showing them both a photo of a flattened city block. "These happen before an earthquake."

Father nodded, a smile spreading across his face. When he looked at me, I felt as if the last few years had washed away and he was putting me to sleep, gently. "Of course it is," he said. "Don't be frightened. I have felt these. They come and go without harm. Here in Turkey it is extremely rare that the foreshocks precede anything serious."

"Is that true, *Baba*?" Osman asked warily.

Father crossed his heart. "Or may the Lord turn me into a warty toad before I say the word *feezborgen*."

"Feezborgen!" Osman and I cried at the same time, and we all dissolved into laughter.

Osman and Father drifted off to sleep almost immediately. And I, dear Diary, am about to follow.

Tuesday morning

SORRY FOR TAKING so long to write, Diary. Since Saturday there have been no more tremors, I'm happy to report. Some of Father's associates have been showing up to the house more and more—the old tomb robbers, Gencer, Ali, Ahmet, and Dodi. They're small-time crooks, making a living (sort of) by scrounging and selling scrap metal, stolen hubcaps, and the like. They've always loved Father's tales of treasure hunting—they've always thought he was some kind of genius. But even with all that activity, it seems that nobody has been able to think of a realistic plan to raise the huge sum Feyyaz is demanding. Honestly, I don't know why he thinks these gap-toothed, unwashed men can help.

It's not just about the money this time, Diary, is it? Father has three days left to think of a plan to save our lives.

Tuesday night

ANOTHER DAY OF Father's team coming in and out has gone and our home is a complete mess again. I give up. If Father wants to live in squalor, so be it.

Osman is getting more and more scared every day. He keeps saying, "I don't want to go work for Feyyaz."

Neither do I, Diary!

Wednesday

LOTS TO TELL.

Too much. My heart is racing, Diary. It's after midnight.

Gencer just left. Father fell asleep with his head on the table, so I've more or less got the room to myself. Osman slept through much of the action. I can't wait to tell him in the morning.

I will go back to this afternoon. Gencer came in, followed by Father's gang. He had a loaf of bread under his arm and a disturbing smile on his face. Well, to be fair, it's disturbing any time Gencer smiles. He plopped the bread on the table and helped himself to a cup of coffee.

"That pot's been there since this morning," Father said. "Let Aliyah make a fresh one, Gencer."

"You haven't seen a morning in years, Khalid," Gencer muttered.

"Ah," Father said, looking hard at Gencer, "no matter. You wouldn't know fresh coffee if it spit in your eye. So, what brings all you gentlemen here? A sudden brilliant plan? Perhaps involving disguises as Arab sheiks—"

"Hear him, Khalid," said Ahmet, a fat man with a ring in his ear. "You would do well to listen."

"I'm all ears," Father said dubiously.

Gencer pulled up a chair and straddled it, leaning forward over the back. "The new museum of underwater archaeology in Bodrum is receiving a load of artifacts in the wee hours Thursday morning. Gold, ancient sculpture, long-lost jewels, treasures from thousands of ancient shipwrecks."

"How do you know this?" I asked.

Gencer scowled at me. "I don't recall asking the children to join the conversation. This is men's business."

Men's business! Just like betrayal and drunkenness, I wanted to say, but Father spoke first. "And men who are not used to planning should listen to girls who do it well," he snapped. "Answer the question. How do you know?"

"Let's say I have a friend in the right place." Gencer paused, staring levelly at Father. "Now, we know Feyyaz is a lover of ancient art and antiques. Even just a few pieces should be enough to get him off all our backs."

Father stiffened. "What are you saying, Gencer? That your . . . friend will skim some objects off the shipment for us?" He looked from one man to the next, his eyes wide with disbelief. "With a cutlass and an eye patch, perhaps? You are consorting with pirates now? This seems too good to be true—we do nothing, your friend does all the work. How do we pay this friend? Where do we meet him? How do we get the goods here from Bodrum? How do we know he's honest?"

"Oh, he's certainly not honest," Gencer said with a leer. "Anyway, when the shipment arrives, there shouldn't be more than a skeleton crew guarding the museum. My man says security's not their top priority . . ."

I've never trusted Gencer, but at that moment I thought he'd gone a bit crazy, too.

"You mean we're going to intercept the shipment?" I blurted out.

"Must she interrupt?" Gencer looked annoyed. "Can she not go to her room?"

"This is my room," I muttered.

"Khalid, with the extra money from this haul, you could buy a house in the country for your children," Gencer said. "Many extra rooms."

"What do you say to my daughter's questions?" Father demanded. "Are you saying we're going to have to cut off the shipment to the museum and take the artifacts by force?"

Gencer's silence was all the answer Father needed.

"Don't you realize there's a reason I rob only old tombs?" Father said. "Do you want me to put my children in direct, mortal danger? We're not fighters, Gencer. We are tomb robbers, not criminals."

"Oh?" Gencer said, staring at Osman and me. "What's really criminal is how you raise your children, living in filth like this."

Dodi gasped.

Father abruptly stood up from the table. He spoke in a low growl. "You'd better get out of my sight before I—"

"Before you what? Kill me?" Gencer said. "We are both dead men when Feyyaz is through with us. Think, Khalid. I know you want something better for your family. This haul will make us all rich, even after we pay off Feyyaz."

Father held Gencer's glance, then turned away. "Tombs are a far different beast from museums. How can we be the right bunch for this? None of us are fighters."

"I'd become a fighter if there was enough money in it," Ahmet said.

"I'd become a fighter for a couple of ounces of gold, at that!" Dodi added.

As the men grunted in agreement, Gencer stood up, looming over Father. "I'm afraid there's no choice, Khalid," he said. "I dearly hope, for the sake of your children, that you're in."

The room fell silent. Everyone looked at Father. I held my breath.

Father's shoulders slumped. He looked suddenly small and old.

"All right," he murmured.

"*Baba*!" Osman and I blurted out.

The other men cheered and broke out a bottle, but Father was still. As he rose from the table, Osman grabbed his hand. I could see he was thinking fast, feeling protective of Father. "We—we will help you, *Baba*," he said.

Father glowered at him in a way I'd never seen. "You two will have nothing to do with this!"

Shaking Osman's hand loose, he went for the door, passing among his thieving, drinking buddies without touching a drop.

I ran after him, afraid of what I might say, but completely aware of how I felt. He was not going to do this without us. "*Baba*, this is suicide," I said, grabbing his hand and spinning him around. "You can't do this with these men."

"Because you don't trust me?" he said. "I am your father, Aliyah!"

"They are drunks and thieves—and so are you!" I blurted out.

As the words left my mouth, I wanted to reel them in, to turn back time. I thought he would hit me or even yell at me. But instead, he nodded. "Yes, Aliyah, you're right."

"And I love you!" I blurted out. "As your oldest child, I demand that you do this with your strongest team, not your weakest."

Father looked up toward the shack. Toward the room of half-witted men already bumping chests and shouting unintelligibly. Standing in the doorway was Osman.

"As your youngest child," he said, "I'm in, too."

Wednesday, 4:53 A.M.

I GOT ABOUT three hours of sleep, Diary.

In a few hours we will set out for Bodrum. Father, Osman, Gencer, and I are going early to scout the castle. Gencer's man told him that security is spotty, because the museum hasn't even been open for a year. From what I've read, it sounds like an incredible collection of objects dredged from the Mediterranean, from ancient ship-wrecks and castles that have fallen into the sea. The British Museum and the Turkish government have teamed up to put thousands of these rescued treasures on display.

What I really want, Diary? To be able to walk among the exhibits like normal people—Father, Osman, and I, spending a day (as paying customers) at the museum. I can just picture Osman, face against the glass like a child, leaping from treasure to treasure.

Wow, I wrote that without even thinking of adding "Mother." Maybe my imagination has finally come to terms with the fact that she's gone.

We'll case the museum while it's still light out. Gencer's man refuses to meet with us in person—he doesn't want to get caught if things go wrong. It's our job to make sure things don't go wrong.

I'm worried, though. None of the gang has had much experience with robberies. Robberies of living people, that is. Gencer keeps reminding us that the museum has done all the hard work for us. No diving to the bottom of the sea for us, no dodging spiders or skeleton hands. All we have to do is be at the museum's back entrance at the right time and take what we need from the truck that will be arriving from the north. Gencer says that the team assigned to protect the truck is usually a group of sleepy archaeologists or just the curator himself with a thermos of coffee.

Father's shouting for us from the door. Osman is wearing underwear on his head and dancing around the room, shooting pretend bad guys with his finger. I need to go.

Thursday evening

EVERYTHING HAS CHANGED, Diary. I'm actually excited for one of Father's plans now. Wait. Let me tell you how it all went down. Eep! I can hardly stop myself from skipping to the end.

Okay. Where did we start? The museum.

We arrived at the museum at around midnight. Father and Gencer went to the front of the building, while Osman and I scoped out the rear loading entrance.

We wandered toward the back of the building. I froze. The watchman wasn't some sleepy archaeologist at all. He had silver hair, but he was a tough-looking man with a big revolver holstered at his side. "Move along, move along! Museum's got a truck coming soon!" he shouted.

"I know!" Osman responded.

I froze.

"You know?" The watchman cocked his head, his eyes bearing into Osman.

"Ay . . . no!" Osman stammered. "Ay, no, we won't

leave! No, it's a free country!"

I tried to play along, pulling his hand. "Behavior issues," I said. "Come, Bartu, behave yourself."

"Bartu?" Osman said.

As I yanked him back into the street, the watchman ran toward us, no longer suspicious but fearful, shouting. A loud horn sounded, practically in my ear. We spun around to see a cargo truck bearing down fast.

Before I could react, I felt Osman pushing me, hard. We both tumbled to the other side of the road as the truck skidded to a stop, hopping the opposite curb.

The driver was yelling, the watchman now blocked from sight. Osman and I ran back around the museum and collapsed against the outer wall, our hearts pounding.

"B . . . B . . . Bartu to the rescue," Osman said.

We waited. We could hear the men cursing us, and we prepared to run. But they never did come after us, so after a few moments we peered around the corner. Several men were unloading crates from the truck now, under the watchful eyes of armed guards.

"One . . . two . . . three . . . four," Osman said. "Four of them, with guns!"

"Gencer didn't say anything about gunmen!" I said. Clearly, Gencer was right that there was some serious money in this operation. It was just that much more of it had gone toward security than we thought.

Osman groaned. "Gencer's IQ is lower than his age . . ."

"No . . . ," I said. Gencer was slimy, but I knew he wasn't dumb. I went back over Gencer's actions over the past week in my head. Giving Father up to Feyyaz's man, rallying Father's team against him. "Is there something he knows that we don't?"

"Like what?" Osman asked.

I couldn't answer him. But this smelled to me like a setup. I just couldn't figure out why.

No time to wonder now. We had to tell the team. Osman and I ran back to Father and Gencer at the entrance to the museum.

As we told them the news about the truck and the armed guards, Father's face went red. "It's over, Gencer," he said softly. "I'm not going in there to get my head blown off. You didn't tell me they would have guns. In fact, you made it seem as if they wouldn't be armed at all."

"So what if they have guns?" After a quick glance around, Gencer opened his coat to reveal two pistols strapped to his ribs. "So do we."

Father's face went pale. "I'm calling it off. Now."

"Oh?" Gencer's smile disappeared. "Did someone die and make you dictator? Let's find the others."

As we stepped around the building, a jackhammer started up. We all jumped.

On the west side of the museum, huge industrial lights

flooded the castle wall with a white glow. A construction team was beginning work on a project. Seeing us, one of the men approached. He wore a hard hat, but his hair was graying and he had little round glasses. About Father's age, I'd say. "This area's off-limits!" He did a little double take at Gencer. "Say, haven't we met?"

"No. Never." Gencer began pulling Father's arm, but he stayed put.

"Ah, thank you, sir," Father said, eyeing a carved stone on the ground. "Good work, I see. Archaeological dig?"

"Come on . . . ," Gencer said under his breath

"No, sir—just repairs," the man said, warming up to Father. There's something weirdly charming about Father when he makes an effort. "This old castle got hit hard by those tremors earlier this week. Several sections of the wall here are quite unstable. And being that we're on a fault line, you can't be too careful."

"That relief," Father said, gesturing toward the carved stone. "Why is it here?"

The man smiled. "A piece of the Mausoleum at Halicarnassus. It fell into ruins, and the medieval Knights of Malta used some of the pieces in the wall of this structure."

"Mausoleum?" Father said. "You seem to know a lot."

"After Mausolus, satrap of Asia Minor," the man replied, his face opening into a huge grin. "As for me, I'm Nigel, one of the curators here at the museum. The tomb was built for him by Queen Artemisia . . ."

"Satrap again," Osman murmured, as Father yammered on and on with the man. I wondered why Father was acting so uninformed. We all knew about the Mausoleum. It was one of Father's favorites, an architectural masterpiece that influenced buildings the world over.

"I probably shouldn't tell you this," Nigel said, "but we've got quite a bit of material here from Halicarnassus. I'm a bit obsessed. They say the world's biggest sapphire was hidden in the ruins, and who wouldn't want to find that?"

As Nigel laughed, I could see Gencer starting to take an interest in the conversation. "The architecture was revolutionary for its time," Nigel went on. "Rather than adorning the structure with images of gods, they used nature, animals, real people. We believe the site was just down the hill from here. As for that"—he gestured to the huge hunk of carved stone—"you might be interested in seeing that bas-relief lying over there."

Gencer stepped in between Father and Nigel. "I think we've got to be going. Some business to attend to —"

"We're going to look at the bas-relief," Father said to Gencer as if he were talking to a child.

We walked closer to the stone. It was a piece of granite, carved with the figure of a long-haired man, clad in intricately carved robes that seemed to turn into clouds around his knees. He was shown reaching out and handing a huge smooth ball to a pair of arms that were cut off by the jagged edge of the wall. The ball was carved deep into the stone, and straight lines radiated away from it at every possible angle.

"Hey, that's Mausolus giving his queen the magical bauble, Father!" Osman cried. "But where is Artemisia? Sir, what happened to the other piece?"

Father smiled at the man and put a friendly arm around his shoulders. He led the man away, flattering him, peppering him with questions, jokes, and slaps on the back. Bits of conversation reached our ears. "Were you part of the excavation . . . Incredible . . . What I wouldn't give to have a job like yours!"

As the curator beamed with pride, Gencer's eyes were slits, his lips tight. Is it bad that I love to see Gencer angry?

Moments later we were at a nearby café, where Gencer's men were waiting for us at a table in the back. Father sat down, smiling. "My friends, we have some bad news and some good news," he began. "First, the bad news. The museum is much more heavily guarded than we thought. I see no way to do what we planned without considerable risk and likely bloodshed."

Ahmet, Dodi, and Ali looked alarmed.

"Don't worry, boys, Khalid's got another great plan!" Gencer drawled sardonically.

Father went on, ignoring Gencer. "My friends, I truly believe this is an even better opportunity for us. Far better. You see, there is a ruined tomb just a few miles out of town that the museum's curator Nigel says is very likely the site of the Mausoleum at Halicarnassus!"

"Of what?" Ahmet said.

"Halicarnassus," Father repeated.

"God bless you!" said Dodi.

"It's not a sneeze, it's a place," Father said. "Here, as a matter of fact. Long before it was Bodrum. Apparently the excavation of this particular ancient tomb had been very unlucky. Cursed, even. As they dug deeper, accidents started to happen. A tunnel collapsed and killed the dig foreman. Several of the workers hallucinated that they were being attacked by rotting, skeletal men. One man was inexplicably burned. There were two earthquakes. At last, the entire operation was called off. Another was planned, but the funding hasn't come through yet. Given the workmanship of the pieces they had unearthed, it seemed likely that there were wonderful treasures buried in the ground at the site, but they had not been found."

"Wonderful treasures?" Gencer seemed intrigued. "Are you sure this isn't a fairy tale?"

"Think, Gencer," Father said. "Hallucinations, collapses, invisible fire. This site was trying to protect itself from invasion. Do you know who looted the museum first?

The British. My friends, this great nation of Turkey has a history stretching back thousands of years. There were times when we ruled the world!"

Ahmet nodded, his brow furrowed like sand dunes. "I remember that from school."

"Didn't know they taught that in first grade," Dodi muttered.

"We have always been the bridge between East and West," Father went on. His eyes glowed and his voice took on a deeper note. "Civilizations have risen, flourished, and fallen here. Who even knows what riches they left behind them? We know of the fabulous things that Western explorers have already found here—the great city of Troy, the golden treasure of Priam—but did we benefit from them? No, my friends, we did not! Our heritage has been stolen from us again and again! Is that right, I ask you? Is it just?"

"No!" Ali roared.

Dodi was shaking his head vigorously. Osman's eyes shone with pride. Even I was finding Father impressive.

"Now we have the opportunity to make our own discovery, to find our own past!" Father leaned forward and lowered his voice to little more than a whisper. "Are we going to let a jewel-filled tomb be found and taken away by Englishmen or Germans? Who has a better right to it, them or us?"

I could see Ahmet, Ali, and Dodi all mentally licking their lips. Father had them in his pocket.

"And what about the curse?" Gencer demanded. "The fire, the hallucinations?"

"Well, if you're looking for fairy tales, Gencer," Father responded with a laugh, "look no further. But who were these men who suffered under this supposed curse? Foreigners, despoilers of Turkish heritage. Don't you think that we Turks would face an entirely different situation?"

"The museum is a sure thing," Gencer said, folding his arms, "not a fairy tale. We know exactly what we're facing there."

"Guns," Dodi muttered. "I don't like guns."

Father clasped Gencer by both forearms. "You know how much I value your input, dedication, and friendship, old boy. So I think about your future. I see a happy Gencer, with money to throw around. Fancy cars! My friend deserves to share in this opportunity. Think. At the very least, we find some valuable stone reliefs that will certainly appease Feyyaz. But we could also find a king's fortune. More money than our children's grandchildren could ever spend. All without firing a single shot."

"I'm for Khalid's plan," Ali declared. "If it doesn't work out, we can always come back to the museum."

"That's right," Ahmet agreed.

Gencer's eyes smoldered. He may have been a hothead, but he knew when he was licked. "When Feyyaz asks," he murmured, "this was your idea."

Friday

AFTERNOON? LATE MORNING? I don't know . . .

Write.

Burn.

Those are my jobs today.

Write because I must. Burn because no one else should.

Father, Osman, and I arrived at the ruins as the sun was setting. Gencer and the others were following in Ali's car, but we got there first.

High on a hill overlooking Bodrum, we could see the lights of the tourist hotels blinking on. The ocean liners docked in the bay softly hummed with the noise of American dance music. The air was hot and heavy. One of those strange, warm October nights. I began to feel pinpricks on the skin of my arms.

"Perfect night for dancing," Father said, hand on his hip, looking over the resort district.

"I think something's wrong with me," Osman said, rubbing his arms, hunching his shoulders to his ears. "I'm feeling goose bumps, but it's really hot outside."

"I feel it too," I said. "It's this place. It's weird."

"Weird places," Father said, "are where the real hauls are." He put an arm around each of our shoulders and steered us toward the ruins.

We agreed to comb the landscape for patches of smooth ground, abandoned tools, uprooted bushes, anything that would give us a clue as to where to start our search. My arms began to prickle again, and as I turned to Osman, he met my gaze. His eyes said, *I'm scared.*

"We'll be fine," I told him softly, as we started forward.

"There!" Osman pointed to a spot on the ground. "Did you see that?"

"See what?" I peered downward but didn't see anything unusual.

"That! That smoke!" He pointed again.

Squinting, I saw a tiny spiral of thin blue wisps emerge from the ground. Then it was gone so fast I wasn't even sure I'd seen it.

"Do you think it's a signal?" Osman said. "An . . . omen?"

"Maybe a party of moles burned a blueberry cake," I said.

But my eyes were focused now on a shallow depression, near where the real-or-imagined smoke had come. A large stone jutted out of the center of it. "What's that?" I murmured.

"A rock?" Osman said.

"I know it's a rock!" I replied. "But it's . . . shaped. By a tool. It looks like a carving."

"Well, whoopee," Osman said. "If it's not gold or silver or platinum, I'm not interest—"

53

But he crept forward with me, giving in to curiosity. A strange mark was carved into the surface of the rock. I stepped forward and reached out to brush some soil from it. "Those tremors last week," I said. "Maybe they caused a small collapse in the ground."

As my finger touched the cold stone, a thunderous groan came from deep within the earth. The ground shuddered and pitched beneath me.

"Aliyah?" Osman's eyes were as wide as saucers. I could see Father running toward me across a field.

I heard a deafening crack, and looked up to see a fir tree falling toward me. I scrambled aside as the trunk hit the ground. Its spidery branches caught my clothes and I stumbled to my knees. As I fell, I felt the ground shudder again. A zigzag opened in the ground between my knees. I heaved myself to the side as the earth ripped apart, spilling soil and gravel downward.

As suddenly as it began, it was over. Everything was silent—but for Osman and Father, both screaming my name. "Here!" I cried out.

Osman clambered over the tree and scrambled to my side. "You're safe!" he said, opening his arms.

"Are you going to hug me?" I replied.

"No!" he shouted. "Why would I—?"

"Dear lord . . . ," came Father's voice from a distance.

He was at the other side of the chasm in the earth—and

only now did I get a sense of its size. Osman and I both craned our necks over the edge of a gash at least twenty feet wide. The last bits of sunlight threw our gigantic, gangly shadows out across the chasm as if we were monsters from the center of the earth.

"Are you both all right?" Father called out, running around the crack toward us.

"Fine," I said.

But Osman was pointing into the darkness. "What's that?"

Father raced to our side, staring downward, too—at what looked like a piece of metal, deep under the ground, catching the last golden rays of sunlight. Although it must have been buried for centuries, it glowed brightly, untarnished. My breath caught in my throat.

"Our mother lode . . . ," Father murmured, as Dodi, Gencer, and the others arrived beside us. Father stared slack-jawed into the hole. "Revealed by the quake as if by magic! It's as if the earth itself wants us to find this treasure . . ."

"I don't see nothing," Dodi said, as the sun's light moved just a fraction of an inch, leaving an inky darkness.

"Men, let's get some ropes," Father said.

"And . . . er, flashlights!" Gencer added, trying to assert some control.

As they raced to get the supplies, Osman squeezed my

hand. "I don't want to go down there."

"What happened to Osman the Brave?" I asked.

"He's being shielded by Osman the Too-Smart-to-Be-Stupid," he replied.

I almost laughed. Osman was right. We were staring into earthquake damage, with no reason to think the quake had ended. But for some reason I felt only an overwhelming excitement.

"It'll be you and me—together," I said. I could feel his fright, but my own skin was tingling with anticipation. "We'll be fine as long as we hang together."

"H-h-hang?" Osman said.

I grabbed him by both shoulders. "We can do this, little brother. We're kids. We move fast. Think about it. We have access to something under here—something that no one has seen for who knows how long. No looters. No pirates. We will be the first. And you know what Father says. The first rule of his business."

Osman nodded. "Finders keepers."

"This could be it, Osman," I said. "No more living in a shack. We can buy things. Go back to school—"

"Whaaat?" Osman looked dismayed.

"Okay, maybe not that," I said. "The point is, we will be in charge of our own destinies! You and me!"

As Osman fell silent, Father's Jeep coughed and sputtered over a pile of rubble, parking a few meters from where we'd seen the glint. He jumped out of the driver's seat and began unloading supplies.

"The others will be here in a moment," he said, heaving a huge coil of rope to the ground. "Are you ready, my little explorers? Remember, two tugs means 'all okay' and three means you need help."

I glanced at Osman. After a long moment, he nodded. We were ready.

"Let's go," I said, holding his hand firmly.

The team arrived just as Osman and I finished looping the dark, heavy rope around our waists. Ahmet's face was ashen. "You kids are—"

"Courageous," Ali cut in.

"Yeah, courageous," Ahmet piped up.

Dodi shrugged. "That wasn't the word I would have chosen—"

His sentence ended in a shout as Gencer poked him in the ribs with his elbow.

Father and Ahmet gave us flashlights and lowered us down into the crack in the earth. After a few meters the crack was narrow enough for Osman and me to brace against each other until we reached the object we'd seen—a metallic opening to a hole in the soil. As I shone my flashlight into the dark, the prickling in my arms grew stronger.

We pushed off the wall of the chasm to stand on the steeply sloping floor of the tunnel. It looked like an old mine shaft, except there were no wooden supports and the walls were eerily smooth. The rope went slack as we found our footing.

I pulled twice on the rope. All clear.

Two gentle tugs from above returned the signal. "Are you all right?" Father's voice echoed down to us.

"There's a tunnel down here!" Osman shouted, deafening me for a moment as his voice was amplified in every direction by the smooth, curved walls.

"What's inside?" Dodi asked.

"How would they know, you fool?" Gencer shot back.

I ducked, walking carefully in, planting my feet to avoid falling. The going was slow, the oppressive heat seeming to intensify the farther belowground we got. As the air thickened I thought we might be getting close to water. My flashlight beam was picking out waves of motion in the air.

Wisps of blue.

I stopped. "Do you see—?"

"It's . . . the blue smoke," Osman whispered. As the earth began to creak and groan, he grasped my hand. His fingers were clammy and wet. A high-pitched noise reverberated through the tunnel. "Bats? Are those bats?"

"Th-they're more afraid of us than we are of them," I muttered.

"Wanna bet?" Osman replied.

Osman turned and shone his flashlight back behind

us. Although we'd only gone maybe twenty yards, the blue smoke had thickened behind us so that it hid the opening of the tunnel. It felt as if we'd been down under the earth forever. I figured Osman wanted to go back.

I have to admit, I was thinking the same thing.

But all he said was, "The walls, Aliyah . . ."

"What?" I replied. "What's happening to them?"

"Not what's happening—what happened," he said. "There's something carved into them."

I turned around to see faint letters in the wall, letters I'd completely missed as we'd walked. "Looks like the same script we saw in the tomb."

As I traced the chiseled lines with a finger, the hairs on the back of my hand slowly rose until they were sticking straight up. "Maybe the name of the dude who built this tunnel," Osman said shakily.

We worked our way slowly forward, down the tunnel, following the lines of text. "That's a long name," I said.

The tunnel suddenly leveled out and we aimed our flashlights straight in front of us. We seemed to be in some sort of chamber. For a moment I had visions of our earlier adventure. I half expected Safi to come running out. But this all changed as my light caught a shape against the wall to my left.

A foot.

Carved into the rock.

We both trained our beams on it, moving them slowly upward, and saw a carving of a gigantic, regal-looking woman standing in the doorway of what seemed to be a Greek temple. Her hair was wavy and wild, blown back by the wind. Her robes were rich and many-layered. The carving was exquisite, showing intricate details of the bangles on her ankles, but her arms . . . were gone. Halfway to the elbow her arms disappeared.

This was the other half of the relief from the museum.

In my head I joined this half of the carving to the one we had seen at the museum. A man, clothed in exotic patterns, with a huge, flowing beard was handing a large ball to this regal woman. Her strong shoulders, her high cheekbones, and her stance said royalty.

"It's the queen," Osman said. "From Father's story."

"How in the world did they get half of this aboveground?" I said.

"Come on," Osman said, tugging my hand. "Let's keep going. The sooner we get to the end of this tunnel, the sooner we can find the queen's treasure."

We picked up the pace, rounding a curve in the tunnel, but it was blocked by a tall stone obelisk leaning diagonally across our path. At its base was a pile of rubble, and at the top were five stone prongs set around the obelisk like a claw.

I could hear the breath catch in Osman's throat. "Do you think that thing—that holder—is where they kept the

Big Bahooley? The sapphire?"

A glint of light from the rubble beneath the structure caught my eye. Osman saw it, too, and leaped forward, brushing away bits of soil and rock.

"Oh . . . my . . ." The words caught in his throat. In his hand was a solid ball of blue bigger than his head, of such brightness that it seemed to explode my flashlight beam into a prism of pulsing light. It was covered in an intricate filigree that seemed to shift in color as I moved my head. Gold? Silver? I couldn't tell, but I could feel my face flush as I stared at it.

An uncontrollable giggle bubbled up out of Osman's throat. I tilted my head back and let out a whoop, barely able to control my own body movement. I was twitching, dancing, jumping like a baby. "We found it!" I shouted up the tunnel. "We found it!"

No answer.

"We're too far," Osman said. "Let's bring it back."

Seizing the rope at my waist, I tugged on it four times. I pictured Father and his men scrambling to their feet, never expecting to feel the victory signal.

I waited to feel two tugs in response, but they didn't come. Was the rope caught on something, perhaps? I turned and shone my flashlight up the tunnel the way we had come.

And I gasped.

Wreathed in wisps of blue smoke, a gaunt, wrinkled woman stood in the tunnel, holding the severed end of the rope in her hand. Her skin was like peeling leather, and her long, silver-and-black hair lay crazy and unkempt over her shoulders. Her lidless eyes blazed with anger.

"Visitors for Artemisia?" Her voice seemed to emanate from deep within the earth, raspy and dry like a thousand chittering insects. "How fortuitous."

Artemisia.

I forced myself to stare into her skeletal, decrepit face, imagining the skin smooth, the hair dark.

"It's . . . the queen," Osman whispered. "From the legend."

Somehow, we had . . . what? Awakened her? Summoned her? Whatever we had done, she wasn't happy.

I felt the earth shake again. I wanted us to run, but my whole body was frozen in place. Was I under a spell? Stiffened by fear?

"Pray tell, how did you get here?" Artemisia demanded. She was staring intently at Osman. "And . . . what is this I sense? Have you the mark, young man?"

"The . . . what?" Osman said. "Marker? You need to do some writing? Sure. I think we—"

"The mark! And you will address me as My Queen!" Artemisia's scream pierced my ears like a rapier. As Osman turned away, I sank to my knees in pain.

"You are young," Artemisia said, staring at the back of my brother's head, "but, yes, I see it forming. Very good."

"I don't know what you're talking about," Osman said. "But we're sorry. My Queen."

"Very sorry, My Queen," I agreed. "Super sorry."

"Here!" Osman sputtered, holding the blue bauble out toward Artemisia. "I wasn't going to take it anyway. Um, we were just checking out your, uh, cool tunnel here and we were about to head home."

"You think you can just walk out of here?" She reached her bony hand toward my brother's chest, her fingers crooked like talons. "When I haven't fed in years?!" The blue gas gathered around her fingers, pulsing with light.

Osman dropped the blue ball. His body began to quiver, his chest heaving.

What was she doing to him?

I snapped out of my frozen state. "Stop! What are you doing? He's a kid! He has nothing for you!"

She paused and looked at me. "What did you say?"

"My Queen!" I added.

"Are you saying this boy has no soul?" Artemisia asked. "How can that be?"

I nearly fell back on my heels. Was that what she was after—Osman's soul?

"His . . . soul belongs to him," I said. "It's not removable, like a fingernail."

"Don't give her any ideas!" Osman screamed.

"I am old," Artemisia said, "but, like you, I must be fed. And I will be fed."

Osman was rising off the ground, his mouth forming an oval of shock. The queen was closing her eyes now, smiling.

"WAIT!" I ran between them and felt a jolt, as if I'd stuck my entire torso into an electric socket.

Artemisia's eyes blinked open, and the shock drained. "Are you offering, also?" she asked. "That is generous."

"No!" I squealed. "I mean, yes!"

"Yes?" Artemisia said, turning her face toward me.

"Why settle for two . . . young souls?" I improvised. "You know, immature, unformed. We have . . . more souls available. Fine, aged souls."

Osman looked at me in shock. I knew it sickened him that I was saying these words. Offering other people. Volunteering other lives.

I tried to send him a mental message. I am bluffing. To get out of here.

"Oh . . . oh, yeah!" Osman said. "A—a bunch of them! Grown men! Big and juicy souls!"

"Is this true? How can I believe you? I see no others." Artemisia cocked her head and the blue smoke withdrew from her hand. "What power have you to offer the souls of others?" she asked. I thought of offering Gencer to Artemisia, leaving with the jewel, rejoicing with Father.

Osman looked at me, then back at her. "Because . . . um, I have . . . the mark! That's it. I'm the Chief Assistant Officer of Bartevyan Antiquities, Inc.! I'm actually older than I look. And I can get my employees down here, all soulful and all. They're going to want a price, though."

"What price?" Artemisia asked.

"That blue soccer ball–looking thingy, " Osman said.

Artemisia's eyes burned white hot, and the blue smoke around her began circling her body, a living wreath of smoke. Waves of heat blasted my face as she approached. "Do you think I care about that godforsaken ball? I can't wear it. It is a key to nothingness. This is hardly a fair trade. But if it's what you want, I think we might have a deal."

Osman and I stood, mouths open, rooted to the spot. Was it really going to be that easy? I guess hundreds of years underground doesn't make you a good negotiator.

"Go now before I change my mind!" Artemisia shrieked, ripping our eardrums to shreds.

Osman grabbed the orb. We started toward the severed end of the rope that led to the surface. I reached for it.

Then it moved.

Was Artemisia playing tricks on us?

I heard a thump, and another. Heavy footsteps approached as the end of the rope slid back into the darkness. Then Father appeared, lit only by the dim blue light of Artemisia's smoky armor.

"You're alive!" Father gasped. "And . . ." His voice dried up as he saw Artemisia.

"Thank you, boy," she said. "This man's soul will tide me over until you bring me the rest."

I realized what we had just done. Osman shook his head. "No," he said. "You can't do this."

"Osman . . . ?" Father said, his eyes widening.

Artemisia reached a clawlike hand toward him. With surprising gentleness, she laid it against his chest. Father looked uncertain. Then he knew exactly what was happening. As the life flowed from him, his eyes met mine. *Go!* he mouthed.

But I froze in horror as a flash of light burst from his chest. He shuddered, his eyes rolled back in his head, and his knees buckled.

Before our eyes he crumpled to the ground, lifeless and inert.

Osman screamed. My mouth hung open as my brain searched for a way to react. Bitter bile rose in my throat. I felt like I was going to be sick.

Father's body was drained of all color, a rag doll left on the floor, as if it had never been alive. Never been that enthusiastic, foolish man, leaping for joy at the news of some distant treasure, rubbing his hands as he crafted another misguided plan, smiling all the while.

"Father!" Osman moaned, tears cascading down his cheeks.

I tried to scream, to cry, but my body seemed like it was no longer mine, frozen by the sight of my father lying on the ground like a pile of old clothes.

Artemisia, however, was a changed woman. Her wrinkled skin was no longer cracked, her shoulders no longer stooped. Through the fog I noticed that her hair had more black than gray in it now. Her voice was clearer, healthier.

"Thaaank youuu," she said.

She grinned widely, and her head tipped back as she began to rise off the tunnel floor.

Osman looked up from Father's side, face streaked with tears. His lips bunched together, his hands shook. "You're not a queen!" he screamed, "You're a killer! You're a witch!" But Artemisia was oblivious to his cries. She floated there, blissfully ignoring us.

This was our chance. I shook free of my trance, blinking back tears, and tucked the ball under my arm. "Let's go!" I cried, starting toward the end of the tunnel.

"I'm coming." Osman knelt at Father's side, trying to lift the body into his arms.

Osman might have grown up that day, but he was still no match for the dead weight of a grown man. "Leave him, Osman! We have to go. Now!" I screamed.

Sobbing, Osman let go and we began scrambling up the steep tunnel.

I found the severed rope and gathered it in my hands,

yanking as hard as I could. I shouted wordlessly up the tunnel, hoping desperately that Father's team had enough loyalty to wait for him to return.

I felt a tug on the rope and relief washed over me. We were going to make it. I could see pale light at the end of the tunnel. Daylight. I held on to the rope as Ali and Ahmet hauled me up.

As I reached for Osman's hand, I heard a rushing noise, like a waterfall. A billow of hot air hit us from below.

"MINE!" Artemisia's voice erupted from the tunnel. At the same moment, Osman's hand jerked out of my grasp.

"Aliyah!" Osman screamed.

Then he was gone, snatched backward into the dark. Loose soil and stones rattled after him, a small avalanche, blocking the mouth of the tunnel.

And then . . . silence.

The queen of the underworld was gone.

Osman was gone.

Father was gone.

All I had left was the blue bauble from the legend.

I stared at it as tears welled up and blinded me. "No," I screamed, but my throat was too dry to make a sound.

My eyes are closing, Diary. I need a few minutes of rest before I—

Friday evening

I'M AWAKE AGAIN.

I wish I were dreaming, Diary, but there's more to tell.

Hands reached down into the tunnel and pulled me up after a minute or two of climbing. I crawled onto solid ground. Gencer gasped and snatched the blue bauble out of my hands. The men cheered and crowded around him.

I burst into tears.

"What's wrong with you?" Gencer asked. "Where's Khalid and your brother? What happened?"

"Sh-she took them," I sobbed. "Artemisia!"

"Arte-who?" Ahmet said.

"You were right here! We weren't more than twenty meters away! You didn't hear anything?" I screamed, falling to my hands and knees. Sobs racked my body.

"All we heard was you shouting Osman's name." Gencer shook his head.

"She took them both—Father and Osman," I said.

"What do you mean? Who is she? Are they alive?" Gencer said.

I shook with anger. "The Queen of the Underworld. Artemisia. She's down there—and she took my brother!" Suddenly a thought struck me. How could I have been so stupid! "Maybe it's not too late! She said Osman had some sort of . . . mark . . . maybe she's not going to rip out his soul so fast. If we hurry maybe we can . . ."

There was a booming sound from deep inside the tunnel. I knew my plea would go unanswered but I tried anyway. "Ahmet? P-please?" My voice broke.

The men exchanged glances.

"I'm not going down there, I won't fit," Ahmet said.

"The tunnel is completely blocked," Dodi added.

"Khalid should never have gone down there," Ali said. "Is this the curse Nigel talked about?"

"I warned him," Gencer sighed, shaking his head. "I told him it was a bad idea."

I turned away, sickened, as one by one Father's friends abandoned him.

For a piece of jewelry.

A fortune, yes, but was it worth it?

They think so, but they didn't just lose their whole family.

I can't even think about tomorrow, Diary. I am lost.

Saturday

I DON'T KNOW if I slept or not. Or if I ever will again. All I know is that I am wrapped in Father's military coat. My arms are stiff, my back bruised. No one remains. The blue bauble is gone, too.

I have scoured the earth for the gash, but it, too, has disappeared as if it never existed.

So this is it, Diary. Today I bury you and start a new life. Today I am alone.

I will embrace Alone. Alone will be my ally. If you have no one, then you have nothing to lose.

I know Artemisia is down there. I can feel her through the earth. She may think she has the souls of my father and my brother. But she is wrong. I have them. My mother's, too, deep inside me. In a way the zombie queen could never understand.

I am all of them. And I will have my revenge.

My vow:

I will track down that scum, Gencer, and get the jewel back. It might well have magical powers, and if it does I will find out how to use them. I will become rich, powerful, and influential. Gencer will wish he'd never met my father and my family.

And then I will teach Artemisia the meaning of pain.

Dear Diary, I know now that my brother had the mark. I will find out what that is. I know this blue ball is the key to more than nothingness. My father and brother will not have died in vain. I will make their lives mean something.

This is my solemn promise. Even if it takes all of eternity.

—Aliyah

READ A SNEAK PEEK OF BOOK FOUR

SEVEN WONDERS

THE CURSE OF THE KING

LEAVING THE LOCULI at home was out of the question. Dad and I were both paranoid the Massa—or some snoop hired by Morty Reese—would break in and steal them. So we took them with us on Dad's jet. For protection.

The ride was bumpy. We argued for six hours about how to proceed. Aly was still thin and quiet from being sick. But by the time we reached the Kalamata Airport, we had a plan. Cass, Aly, and I would grab a taxi. Alone. Bringing Dad with us, we decided, would make the Massa suspicious.

So we left him and the Loculi behind in the plane.

I was a nervous wreck.

The taxi had no air-conditioning and a hole in the front passenger floor. Rocks spat up into the car from the road as we drove. As we sped noisily across Greece, the mountains of the Peloponnese rose up in the distance to our right. And Cass had a revelation. "Whoa," he cried out, looking up from his phone. "The meaning of *Roudouni* is *nostril*!"

"Is geography!" our driver said. (Everything he said seemed to come with an exclamation point.) "Just north of Roudouni is long mountain with—how do you say? Ridge! To Ancient Greeks, this looks like straight nose! Greek nose! Strong! At bottom is two valleys—round valleys! Is like, you know . . . *thio roudounia* . . . two nostrils!"

"And thus," Cass announced, "Roudouni *picked* its name."

"Cass, please . . ." Aly said.

Cass began narrating like a TV host. "Our car develops a moist coating as it enters the rim of the *roudouni*. It is said that the people here are a bit snotty, tough around the edges but soft at the core."

"Ha! Is funny boy!" the driver exclaimed.

Cass gestured grandly out the window. "Exotic giant black hairs, waving upward from the ground and dotted with festive greenish globs, greet visiting tourists as they plunge upward into the—"

"Ew, Cass—just *ew*!" Aly said. "Can we leave him by the side of the road?"

On the outskirts of town, goats roamed in vast, sparse fields. Old men in ragged coats stared at us, their backs bent and their hands clinging to gnarled wooden canes. Black-clad old ladies sat knitting in front of rickety shacks, and a donkey ignored our driver's horn, just staring at us in the middle of the street. I felt strangely paranoid. I clutched the backpack tightly.

As we drove slowly through a flock of squawking chickens, I read the English section of a big, multilingual road sign:

YOU ARE APROCHING ROUDOUNI

THE PRID OF THE PELOPONNESE!!!

"Prid?" Cass said.

"I think they mean 'pride,'" Aly answered.

Where on earth *were* we?

"Maybe we should have brought Dad along," I said. "This is pretty remote."

"We want the Massa to think we're alone," Aly said. "That was the plan. If we need to, we can call him."

I nodded. Dad had promised to hire a chopper if necessary, if anything were to go wrong. Which seemed weird, considering that "going right" meant being captured.

I tried to imagine Brother Dimitrios and his gang actually traveling to this place. I couldn't imagine *anyone* in his right mind traveling here.

We rounded a bend, following a narrow alley lined with whitewashed buildings. The car began swerving around potholes, bouncing like crazy. "Who paved this road," Aly grumbled, "Plato?"

"Is funny girl!" the driver barked.

He slowed to ten kilometers an hour as we crept toward the town center. I knew we were getting close by the sound

5

of Greek music and the smell of fried food. Soon the dark, tiny street opened up into a big cobblestoned circular plaza surrounded by storefronts. We paid the driver and got out. I don't what they were cooking, but I had to swallow back a mouthful of drool.

Did I say I was starving?

I was starving. I hadn't eaten in five hours.

Most of the shops were shuttered for the night, but the cafés and restaurants were jumping. People strolled across the plaza, slowly and aimlessly, arm in arm. Kids chased each other and played catch. In the restaurants, stray cats wove around people's legs, looking for scraps, while entertainers in flowing costumes sang and played tambourines, guitars, and strange instruments that sounded like oboes. Old men sat silently outside the cafés at backgammon tables, sipping coffee and amber-colored drinks. An outdoor bar called AMERICA!! had two huge flat-screen TVs, one blaring a soccer game in Greek and the other an old rerun of *Everybody Loves Raymond* in English.

In the center was Zeus.

Or something Zeus-ish.

The statue glowered over the surroundings like a creepy, unwanted party guest. No one seemed to be paying it much notice. Its face and shoulders were peeling and pockmarked, like it had a skin disease. Its eyes were pointed in the direction of a flat-screen TV. Over time the eyeballs had eroded, so it looked like a grown-up Child of the Corn. In its raised hand was a big soccer-ball-like thing, but I could barely see it under a dense crowd of birds.

"The Loculus of Pigeon Droppings," Cass mumbled, as we slowly walked around the plaza. I could feel the curious eyes of the café-dwelling old men. One of the musicians moved toward us through the crowd—a girl about our age, maybe a little older. The hem of her skirt was raggedy, but the fabric was a rich patchwork of reds, purples, and blues, spangled with bright baubles. Her ankles and wrists jangled with bracelets. As she caught my eye, she smiled and then said, *"Deutsch? Svenska? Eenglees?"*

"Uh, English," I said. "American. No money. Sorry."

One of the café waiters came running toward us, shouting at the beggar girl to chase her away. As she ran off, he gestured toward the café. "Come! Eat! Fish! Music! I give you good price!"

Now customers and coffee sippers were staring at the commotion. "This is bad," I whispered. "We don't want to attract public attention. This is not how you stage an abduction. Kidnappers need quiet."

"Don't look now," Cass said, "but they're here. Other side of the plaza. We're six o'clock, they're twelve. Just to the left of the big TV!"

The TV was no longer playing *Everybody Loves Raymond* but an old black-and-white episode of *I Love Lucy*.

Sitting at a small round table were four men in brown monk robes.

The Massarene.

I couldn't tell if they were the exact same goons who'd tried to kill us in Rhodes. We were too far away. Those pious robes hid a gang of thugs who would shoot at thirteen-year-old kids from helicopters.

"What do we do?" Aly asked.

"They tried to murder us once already!" Cass said.

"That was before the Massa knew who we were," I said. "Remember, they need us."

"So we just walk up to their tables?" Cass asked. "Like, '*Yia sou*, dudes! Can we offer you some baklava for dessert, or maybe a kidnapping'?"

"Just let them see us," I said. "Come on, follow me."

The shortest route was directly across the plaza. People crisscrossed back and forth in front of us, as the sitcom's laugh track washed over the town square. The monks were eating and talking quietly, ignoring the TV. As we passed the statue, one of them looked up toward us. He had a thick brown unibrow and an intense, angry stare.

Aly tugged at my arm. "Where's Cass?"

I whirled around. I could see Cass a few feet behind us, at the base of the statue. He was helping up a crying little boy who had fallen on the cobblestones. The kid's parents smiled and thanked him, jabbering away in Greek. Cass backed away and tripped over a stone, too, landing against the statue. It looked like he was doing it on purpose, to cheer up the little boy and make him laugh. "I'll get him," I said.

But as I stepped toward Cass, I heard an odd cracking noise, like the turning of an ancient mill wheel.

The little boy shrieked, jumping into his father's arms. I could hear chairs scraping behind us, people screaming.

Pop! A jagged projectile of broken stone flew toward me and I ducked.

Pop! Pop! Pop! They were flying all around now.

I scrambled backward toward the café. The monks had left their seats and were backing away. Desserts and dinners lay abandoned on tables, dropped to the ground.

"Jack!" Cass screamed.

High above him, the statue of Zeus turned, shedding more marble pieces. And it reared back its spear, pointing it toward Cass.

"CASS, GET AWAY from it—it thinks you're trying to steal the Loculus!" Aly screamed.

She dove toward Cass, pulling him away from the statue.

Zeus was moving by centimeters. With each jerk of his arm, the marble encasing him cracked . "Lll . . . oc . . . ul . . . ssss . . ."

The word was just barely recognizable. Each syllable was accompanied by a sickening creak.

"Um . . . um . . ." I crawled backward. My tongue felt like a slab of Velcro.

I heard a chaos of noise behind us. Screams. Chairs clattering to the pavement. Children crying. The square was clearing out. Aly clutched my left arm, Cass my right.

Within minutes, the square had completely emptied. No more old men. No bumbling waiters. No begging gypsies or Bouzouki-playing musicians. Just us, the sound of *Family Guy* now on the TV, and the deep groan of the marble cracking.

A mist swirled up from the ground now in tendrils of green, yellow, and blue. It gathered around the statue, whistling and screaming.

The statue's expression was rock-stiff, but its eyes seemed to brighten and flare. With a *pop* of breaking stone, its mouth shot open, and it roared with a sound that seemed part voice, part earthquake. The swirls sped and thickened, and in moments Zeus was juddering as if he had been electrocuted by one of his own thunderbolts.

In that moment we could have run.

But we stayed there, bolted to the spot by shock, as a bright golden-white globe landed on the stones with barely a sound and rolled toward a café. Its surface glowed with an energy that seemed to have dissolved the centuries of grit and bird droppings. I felt my body thrumming deeply, as if each artery and vein had been plucked like a cello.

"The Song of the Heptakiklos . . ." I said.

"So it *is* a Loculus!" Aly said.

I couldn't take my eyes from the orb. I staggered toward it, my head throbbing. All thoughts were gone except one: *If we could rescue Health—with this, we would have four.*

"Jack, what are you doing?" Cass screamed.

I felt Aly grabbing me by the arm, pulling me away. We rammed into Cass, who was frozen in place, staring at the statue. We all looked up. Before our eyes, the statue's veins of marble turned blue and red, slowly assuming the warm, fluid shape of human skin.

Zeus was shrinking. The massive statue was becoming a man.

Or maybe a god.

As the mist receded, Zeus lowered his head. His eyes were a deep brown now, his face dark and his hair iron gray. The muscles in his arms rippled as he stepped toward us, lifting the scepter high above his head. "Loculus . . ." he murmured.

"Give it to him!" Cass screamed. "He doesn't see it! He thinks you stole it! *Yo! Zeus! Your godliness! O Zeus! Look—it's on the ground!*"

"He doesn't understand English!" Aly said.

"*IIII'LL GUB YOUUUU MY PITTTTY!*" the statue bellowed.

"That sounds like English!" Cass said. "What's he saying?"

"Wait. 'I'll get you, my pretty'?" Aly said. "From *The Wizard of Oz*?"

I have no idea why I wasn't running away. But it was moving so slowly, creakily. It clearly hadn't moved in a long time and its eyesight wasn't good. I had no intention of backing away. I wanted that Loculus. "Guys, I'm going after it. Back me up. Distract Zeus."

"Are you out of your mind?" Cass screamed. "We came here to be kidnapped!"

"We came here to win back our lives," I said. "Who knows if we'll ever have this chance again? *Back me up!*"

"But—" Cass stammered. Aly placed a hand on his shoulder. Stepping between Cass and the statue, she straightened herself to full height. "Yo! Lightning Boy!"

The statue turned to face her.

And I moved slowly, step-by-step backward, through the shadows, toward the Loculus. The statue's eyes didn't waver from Aly. He was speaking a string of words in a strange language. It sounded vaguely Greek, of which I understand exactly zero, but the rhythms of it seemed weirdly familiar. Like I could hear the music but couldn't identify the instruments.

Go, McKinley. Now.

I turned. The pale moonlight picked up the contour of the fallen orb in the shadow of a café. As I crept closer, my head was jammed up with the Song of the Heptakiklos now. Gone was the noise from the TVs, from Aly's conversation. The Loculus was calling to me as if it were alive. As I reached for it, I heard something behind me, in a deep, growly rasp.

"OHHHH, LUUUUCY, YOU ARE IN BIIIIG TROUBLE NOW."

I turned. Aly and Cass were both gawking at the statue. "Could you repeat that?" Aly said.

The statue lifted one leg and hauled it forward. It

thumped to the ground. "*TO THE MOOOON, ALIIICE!*"

"What's he saying?" Cass asked.

"*I Love Lucy*," Aly said. "*The Honeymooners*. Those . . . those are lines from old sitcoms."

From behind me came the sound of a laugh track. "That TV . . ." I said. "Zeus has been watching it for years. Decades. It's the only English he knows. The sitcoms and the ads."

The former statue was staring at me now. Its pupils were dark black pools. The muscles in its face seemed to be tightening, its mouth drawing back. As I grabbed the Loculus, I felt a jolt up my arm, as if I'd stuck my finger in an electric socket. I tried to hold back a scream, gritting my teeth as hard as I could.

"Jack!" Aly screamed.

I turned just in time to feel a whoosh against my cheek. Zeus's scepter flew past me, embedding itself in the ground.

Holding tight to the Loculus, I ran for the edge of the town square. In a moment Aly and Cass were by my side. "Follow me!" Cass shouted, leading us down an unlit alleyway.

As we raced out of town, I could see pairs of eyes staring at us out of darkened windows. Mothers and fathers. Children.

A voice behind us thundered loudly, echoing against the stucco walls. "*LOOOOCUULUUUUS!*"